MY BUSHFIRE DIARY

Alan Trussell-Cullen

Australia • Brazil • Japan • Korea • Mexico • Singapore • Spain • United Kingdom • United States

My Bushfire Diary

Fast Forward
Purple Level 20

Text: Alan Trussell-Cullen
Editor: Cameron Macintosh
Design: Vonda Pestana
Series design: James Lowe
Production controller: Seona Galbally
Photo research: Fiona Smith
Audio recordings: Juliet Hill, Picture Start
Spoken by: Matthew King and Abbe Holmes

Acknowledgements
The author and publisher would like to acknowledge permission to reproduce material from the following sources: Photographs by AAP Image/AP Photo/Rohan Sullivan, p 8; Auscape International/David W Hardin, p 22 /Jean-Marc La Roque, p 21 /Jean-Paul Ferrero, p 6 /Wayne Lawler, p 5; iStockphoto.com, p 9 /Henk Badenhorst, p 12 /Kurt Gordon, pp 8-9; Newspix/AFP Photo/John Gress, p 19 /AFP Photo/Pedro Armestre, front cover /Pedro Armestre, p 11 /Chris Crerar, p 15 bottom /Dean Marzolla, p 17 /Gary Graham, p 7 /Jeremy Piper, p 10 /Kristi Miller, p 23 /Mike Ross, pp 3, 16 /Richard Cisar-Wright, p 15 top /Rohan Kelly, pp 14, 18; Photolibrary.com/Ted Mead, p 13 /Botanica/Samuelson Jeremy, pp 4, 20.

ISBN 978 0 17 012662 5
ISBN 978 0 17 012657 1 (set)

Cengage Learning Australia
Level 7, 80 Dorcas Street
South Melbourne, Victoria Australia 3205
Phone: 1300 790 853

Cengage Learning New Zealand
Unit 4B Rosedale Office Park
331 Rosedale Road, Albany, North Shore NZ 0632
Phone: 0508 635 766

For learning solutions, visit cengage.com.au

Printed in Australia by Ligare Pty Ltd
6 7 8 9 10 11 12 20 19 18 17 16

Evaluated in independent research by staff from the Department of Language, Literacy and Arts Education at the University of Melbourne.

My Bushfire Diary

Alan Trussell-Cullen

Contents

Thursday, 3 February

We live on the edge of a small town north of Sydney.
Our house looks out across bush and a gum tree forest.

We haven't had much rain this summer,
so the forest is very dry.
Everyone is worried about bushfires.
People keep asking, "Will this be one of those years?"

I hear so much about bushfires
that I've decided to keep my own diary
over the summer.

For weeks, the forest workers were clearing firebreaks with bulldozers. A firebreak is a gap made in the forest to help stop fire spreading.

Before our town got so big,
the forest workers used to burn off parts of the forest
in winter so there would be gaps
to stop any summer bushfire spreading.
This is called a "controlled burn".

In the last few years,
people have built houses near the forest.
This has made it dangerous
to do any more controlled burns.

Running Words 152

Monday, 7 February

Our teacher talked to us about bushfires today.
She said that bushfires need:

1. **Fuel** like dry grass, plants and trees
2. Oxygen
3. Heat to start the fire.

She said many bushfires are started when people are careless with fires or cigarettes.

Lightning can start a bushfire, too.
We get lots of lightning storms around Sydney.

Our teacher also showed us a **wildfire** map of the world.
Wildfires are fires that burn out of control.
In some places, there are grass wildfires,
while in other places, there are forest wildfires.
And in other places, like where I live,
there are bush wildfires.

the world's wildfires on 31 January, 2007

Chapter 3

Friday, 11 February

This morning, as I was getting on the school bus, I saw smoke.

The bus driver said there was a small fire at Butterfly Creek, about ten kilometres away. We saw fire trucks and tankers rushing to the fire.

The firefighters worked all day
to bring the fire under control.
They put water on the fire and did backburning,
which is when firefighters light small fires
ahead of the big fire.
When the big fire gets to the burnt part,
it can't go any further because there's nothing to burn.

Chapter 4

Saturday, 12 February

This morning, I heard helicopters.
Yesterday's backburning didn't work,
and the fire was bigger.
The firefighters were filling **monsoon buckets**
in the river and dropping the water on the fires.

I saw lots of birds flying away
from the forest.
Bushfires are bad for birds and animals,
as well as trees.

Chapter 5

Sunday, 13 February

Today, the fire went from bad to worse!
It became a crown fire,
which means that the treetops started burning.
Bushfires usually start out as ground fires
and burn slowly.
When the fire gets to the treetops,
it can jump from tree to tree and spread very quickly.

The wind changed, too.
It blew the fire towards the town,
and the air was full of smoke.

The fire could spread towards our house,
so Dad cleared everything away
from around the house
and removed all the leaves
in the gutters.

Chapter 6

Monday, 14 February

Today the police said the fire was coming our way.
We had to leave our house!

We only had time to throw our special things in the car, like photo albums.
I looked after our two cats in the back seat.
My baby brother was crying.

Dad took off from our house fast,
and we went to stay with friends in town.
I couldn't stop thinking about our house
and wondering if it would be there
when the fire was over.

Chapter 7

Tuesday, 15 February

I didn't go to school today or yesterday,
but when we woke up this morning,
there were clouds in the sky –
real clouds, not clouds of smoke!
Later, it started to rain –
our first heavy rain for two years!

We ran outside and danced in the rain
with the firefighters.
We loved that rain because it helped to put the bushfire out.

The firefighters still have to spend another five days damping down **hot spots** to make sure the bushfire doesn't start up again. But yes, the bushfire is over!

Chapter 8

Wednesday, 16 February

Today, we were told we could go back
to our house.
We were worried about what we would find.

No one spoke as we drove up the road.
Then, when we came around the corner,
we saw our house!
The fire missed us.
The firefighters said the wind changed
at the last minute,
which helped to save our house.

Yes, our house was still standing,
but this was what the forest looked like!

Chapter 9

Thursday, 28 December

After the fire,
I forgot all about my bushfire diary.
I found it today in a drawer, and read it.

Lots of things have happened since the bushfire.

New trees have grown
in the ashes of the old trees.
The animals have come back, too.

It's taken many months,
but everything is almost back to normal!

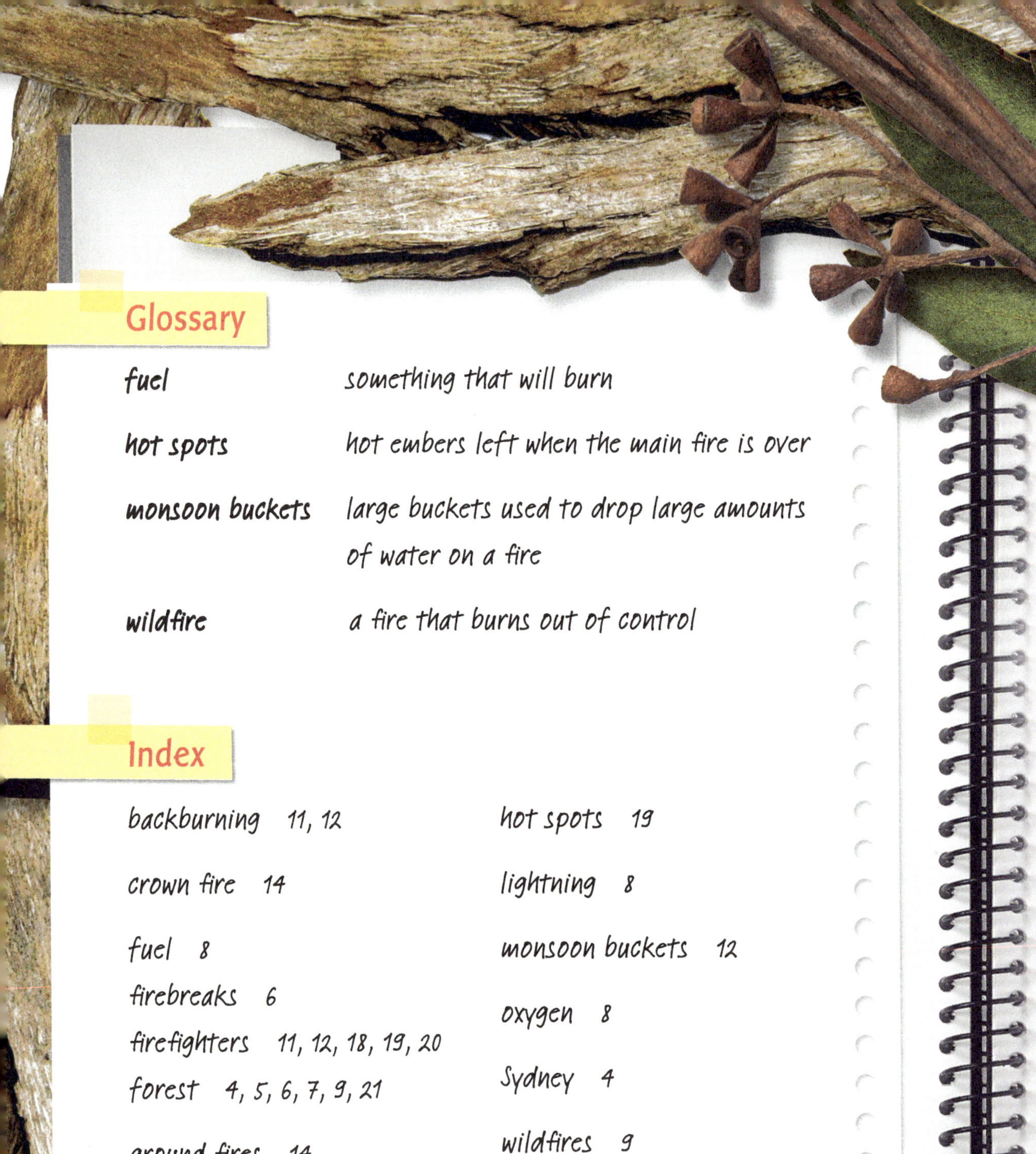

Glossary

fuel	*something that will burn*
hot spots	*hot embers left when the main fire is over*
monsoon buckets	*large buckets used to drop large amounts of water on a fire*
wildfire	*a fire that burns out of control*

Index